The FROGS of BETTS

JEN McVEITY

Illustrated by

TERRY DENTON

 sundance

Published by
ndance Publishing
   lor Street
   , MA 01460

   ight © text Jen McVeity
Copyright © illustrations Terry Denton
Project commissioned and managed by
Lorraine Bambrough-Kelly, The Writer's Style
Designed by Cath Lindsey/design rescue

First published 1997 by
Addison Wesley Longman Australia Pty Limited
95 Coventry Street
South Melbourne 3205 Australia
Exclusive United States Distribution: Sundance Publishing

ISBN 0-7608-1932-7

Printed In Canada

CONTENTS

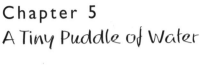

CHAPTER 1

The Last Great Mystery of the World

"Professor Betts, Professor Betts!"
Marchella, the new young assistant, called.
"The frogs have arrived!"

"At last," exclaimed the Professor. "Place them in the lily tanks. Then make sure you give them plenty of beetles to eat."

"Do you really think the experiment will work?" Marchella asked anxiously.

"Of course." Betts was annoyed. "Can you doubt my success?"

"Oh, no, no!" Marchella cried. "Of course not. But Professor . . . may I ask . . . er . . . just exactly what is the experiment about?"

Professor Betts drew himself up to his full height and then glared up at his assistant. "I am about to prove one of the last remaining mysteries of the world," he said. "Soon people will remember my name forever. I will write books. Have my own TV show. No, my own TV station!"

He stopped, took a deep breath, and his voice rose. "With these few amphibians, I will prove once and for all that frogs croak *before* it rains!"

CHAPTER 2

Do Frogs Nod?

All was quiet in the laboratory. Each morning Marchella entered, switched on the radio, and began to clean out the lily tanks.

Carefully she removed the dried up and mashed beetle wings and threw in fresh food. The beetles scurried frantically.

The frogs hopped slowly and gulped the
new beetles into their mouths.

Then they looked up at the assistant. They still seemed hungry.

"Want some more?" she always asked. And they always seemed to nod in reply.

Professor Betts came into the room in a fresh white coat, his name sewn in large letters on the pocket. "Anything new yet?" he asked.

"No, Professor," Marchella answered. "The frogs have been very quiet." She wiped up a large puddle of water by the radio and swept old beetle wings into the trash.

"Turn up the radio," Betts ordered. "Let's see what the forecast is for today."

. . . the Weather Bureau predicts a dry, sunny day, with north to northeast winds . . .

"Good!" cried the Professor. "This proves that when the weather is good, the frogs are silent. The experiment is going well. Now we must wait until it rains. I am sure the frogs will croak in warning."

"You are so clever, Professor," said
Marchella. "Of course they will croak.
Won't you?" she added to the frogs.

"Er, of course," Betts ran his fingers through his hair. He thought this made him look bold and clever. All it did was give him greasy fingers.

He peered at the frogs gulping steadily on their lily pads. The frogs peered back at him. With their wide mouths and big eyes, they seemed to be grinning.

"Do you realize that if this experiment succeeds, I will be able to predict the weather from just these frogs? From this very room," the Professor announced.

Professor Betts's chest swelled and his words became louder.

"Every satellite will be brought down, weather balloons will no longer exist. All weather forecasting stations will close down. The whole world will wait for my predictions! With these few frogs I will be master of the entire earth!"

"Amazing, Professor. Just amazing!" cried
Marchella.

"Now I have other work to do," the Professor said importantly. "I am working on another vital experiment to discover the average size of the pygmy chimpanzees of Zaire. Continue with your work, Marchella, but call me at once if the frogs start to croak."

CHAPTER 3
TV Frogs and Bogs

The radio continued to predict good weather. Marchella continued to look carefully after the frogs. And the frogs continued to silently squat on their lily pads.

"Any change?" asked Professor Betts, bustling into the laboratory followed by five people with long hair and TV equipment.

"You can plug the cameras in there," Betts
said to them, pointing.

He turned to Marchella again. "Well?" he barked, only it sounded more like a squeak. "I asked about any changes."

"There are none yet," said the assistant. "Except that . . ."

"We're ready to roll," said someone.

A camera started whirring. Betts moved in front of the lily tanks, clearing his throat importantly.

"I believe hogs are far more intelligent than we think," he began.

"Hold it," said the longest-haired man, the director. "Aren't we talking about frogs here?"

"Take two," said someone.

Betts was combing his hair. The frogs looked calm and intelligent in the background. The cameras started filming again.

"I believe frogs are more intelligent when we blink . . ."

"Stop," said the director.

"The lights are not right," said Betts. "They're shining in my eyes."

"Move the lights," someone ordered.

"Take three," someone else called.

"Logs are more . . ." started Betts.

"Take four," called the director.

"Dogs are more . . . I mean, bogs are . . ."

"Take a break, everyone!" The director
stalked out of the room, not looking at
Betts.

"Professor," asked the assistant anxiously, "I was wondering . . . er . . . can the frogs hear us? Can they understand things?"

"They can hear sounds," said the Professor, brushing a tiny crease from his coat. He glanced across at the frogs squatting obediently in their tanks.

"And they know when food is coming. And rain, of course. Maybe even earthquakes. Or cyclones." His fist thudded against the bench. "Floods! Fires!" His fist pounded again and again. "I'll be rich! Rich!"

"Of course, Professor. Of course,"
murmured Marchella. "It's just that . . .
well, when I'm feeding them, or cleaning
out their tanks, the frogs, er . . . sometimes
seem to understand what I say," she ended
with a rush.

"When I said they were intelligent," said Betts coldly, "I didn't mean they were geniuses. They're just frogs. They act on instinct. They have very little brain . . . like you," he added.

"We're ready," a voice called. The director was standing in the middle of the room, breathing slowly and deeply and trying to look calm.

"But, Professor . . ." said Marchella.

"Don't let your imagination run away with you," said Betts firmly. He frowned heavily at his assistant. "You're a scientist," he muttered. "Scientists act only on facts. Do try to remember that."

He turned and faced the cameras again and leaned casually against some test tubes. Glass shattered and bright purple fluid ran everywhere. The cameras didn't stop.

"Frogs are very strange animals . . ." Betts began. He ran his fingers through his hair. They were covered in purple liquid. Purple drops started eating away at his hair. Betts kept on smiling. The cameras kept on rolling.

CHAPTER 4
Birrup, Birrup!

The days dragged slowly by. Marchella washed test tubes and swept floors. She tried to remember that she was a scientist and not to talk to the frogs. But sometimes the words just slipped out.

"Want some more beetles?" she'd croon, and the frogs would blink gratefully. "How about some clean water?" Always, the frogs seemed to smile at her in return.

Then, on the tenth day, a change occurred.

. . . cloud cover increasing and will be followed by rain in the afternoon . . .

"Professor! Professor Betts!" Marchella called. "The weather forecast is for rain. Now is the time to see what the frogs predict!"

The Professor entered quickly, anxious to see what the frogs would do now that rain was forecast.

"Birrup." A tiny croak greeted him from the lily tanks.

"Birrup. Birrup." Another followed, and then another.

"BIRRUP. BIRRUP. BIRRUP." Suddenly, the whole laboratory seemed to be filled with the loud chorus of the frogs. "BIRRUP. BIRRUP. BIRRUP." The air rang with the harsh sounds of their croaking.

"Success at last!" shouted the Professor. "Now my time has come! Riches will be mine forever. Entire countries will be at my feet! I will be the weather forecaster for the whole world!"

"Oh, Professor," Marchella murmured, "you are amazing!"

"Of course," Betts answered. "Come, we must inform the President at once. And after that, the world!"

CHAPTER 5
A Tiny Puddle of Water

It was morning again. The laboratory was deserted. The heavy croaking of the frogs throbbed loudly in the air. "BIRRUP. BIRRUP. BIRRUP."

Unseen by human eyes, a lone frog hopped out of the lily tank and made its way across the counter. It stopped by the radio, waiting, watching. A tiny puddle of water formed. No humans were near.

At last, the frog reached out one webbed foot and turned a dial carefully. The voice from the radio boomed out over the frogs' loud croaking.

. . . the Weather Bureau predicts a clear, mild day, with no rain for the next 24 hours . . .

The frog raised one of its cold, wet feet in command.

"BIRR . . ." Suddenly the harsh croaking ceased. The frogs sat in their tank, silent once more. Heads cocked, grinning to themselves, they settled down to listen to the rest of the news.

About the Illustrator

Photo: Rob Hamer

Terry Denton

Gasp!, Spooner or Later, Duck for Cover, Freeze a Crowd, Felix and Alexander, Mr. Plunkett's Pool, and *The Paw* are some of the books that I have either written or illustrated or both written and illustrated.

My drawings are either very simple, or very detailed, or slightly detailed with simple funny parts, or fairly simple with slightly detailed funny parts.

My writing is much the same, only simpler. In my spare time . . . well, let's face it, I don't have any spare time. And I don't drive a Porsche.

I do have a dog with three legs . . . well, two . . . OK, it's a chicken — but it barks!!

[Bet you haven't got a chicken that barks.]

About the Author

Jen McVeity

A full-time author, Jen McVeity loves illustrators who do either very simple or very detailed drawings or who do very detailed drawings and are simple. All her family and other animals have the right number of legs. She has never lied about her children, her age, or her pets. Well, almost never . . .

She has sixteen books published, five about to be published, and seven that she hopes will be published — if she ever gets around to finishing them. Her next book will probably be about a mad illustrator who can't count and who thinks chickens bark.

Jen has jumped off cliffs, skied glaciers, flown on a circus trapeze, and traveled around the world five times. She calls this research for her writing. Her family calls it having a good time.